THE SILVER CASKET

CHRIS MOULD

Roaring Brook Press

New York

Text and illustrations © 2007 Chris Mould. First published by Hodder Children's
Books, a division of Hachette Children's Books,
an Hachette Livre UK company.
Published by Roaring Brook Press
Roaring Brook Press is a division of Holtzbrinck Publishing
Holdings Limited Partnership
175 Fifth Avenue, New York, New York 10010
www.roaringbrookpress.com
All rights reserved
Distributed in Canada by H. B. Fenn and Company Ltd.
Library of Congress Control Number: 2009933667
ISBN: 978-1-59643-386-1
Roaring Brook Press books are available for special promotions
and premiums.
For details contact: Director of Special Markets, Holtzbrinck Publishers
First Edition April 2009
Book design by MT Dikun
Printed in November 2009 in the United States of America by RR Donnelley
Company, Bloomsburg, Pennsylvania
10 9 8 7 6 5 4 3 2

For Ed Collier Jones

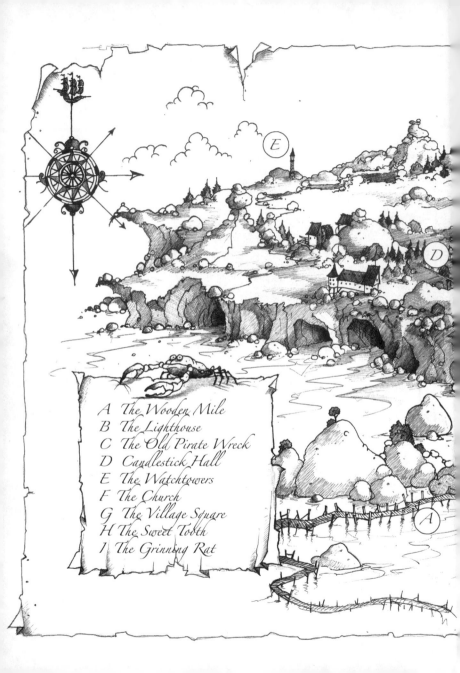

A The Wooden Mile
B The Lighthouse
C The Old Pirate Wreck
D Candlestick Hall
E The Watchtowers
F The Church
G The Village Square
H The Sweet Tooth
I The Grinning Rat

Admiral Swift

The Calm before the Storm

Crampton Rock was still and silent. Early morning light spilled over the horizon onto the harbor. A flock of gulls hitched a ride on the gentle sea breeze, and if you had taken a good look and thought that this place was tranquil and serene, you are easily fooled. Despite the crisp blue sky and golden sands, all hell was about to break loose.

Somewhere far away, a chill wind blew over an old buccaneers' graveyard overlooking the coastline. A handful of crooked tombstones spilled across a grassy knoll.

The turf rippled and beneath it something clawed its way upward.

Pop!

The first of many hands poked its way through the wormy black soil.

Then another. And another, until the festering remains of every grave were shifting silently.

Soon the ragged shapes of men rose above ground, each before his own stone. The men were blackened with clay and soil and were bearing the weapons and wearing the rotted robes that revealed their trade.

"Summon the Devil's Horse," croaked the first one. "She is the best ship for the job."

"Aye, aye sir. So be it" The man carried a bullhorn over his shoulder on a length of rope. He raised it and blew his call. It sailed on the breeze and resounded across the water.

In a short while, the filthy ship would appear, and they would set sail.

Gulls rested on the crowstepped roof of Candlestick Hall. Outside was the soothing view of Crampton Rock harbor, but an argument boiled deep inside its walls.

Mrs. Carelli, the housekeeper, had tracked down the new lord of the manor, young Stanley Buggles. He was in serious trouble and she was hot on his heels.

"I cannot believe the scrapes and situations you have got me into since you inherited this old place, Stanley. We just go from one terrible mess to another. I don't know what your Great Uncle Bart would have thought. He worked hard to shake off his pirate's reputation and live a normal life, and now it's all gone to pot. What will the ladies in the village think?"

"But—" began Stanley.

"We don't never have a moment's peace, and every time I turn my back you've gotten us more nonsense."

"But Mrs. Carelli, I—" Stanley tried.

"This little ol' fishing community lived in

peace on this island before you turned up, Stanley. I'm too old for all this baloney."

"Can I just say something? . . . I—"

"No, you can't. Your precious little Ibis has given us more headaches than it's worth. All that trouble for a silver trinket."

"It is not a trinket." Stanley's voice was raised now. "It has great power! If you ever hold it in your hands you will feel it, just like I did."

"Stanley, listen. It's not that I don't believe you, it's just a little hard to take in," said Mrs. Carelli, holding the boy by his upper arms and staring deep into his eyes. "I want you to explain it to me again. Now, take it slowly."

Stanley paused to collect his thoughts.

"When I first came to Candlestick Hall I found the Ibis nestled in the belly of the preserved pike in his glass case on the wall.

The Ibis looked beautiful as I held her in my hands. There was no way I could have known, but in touching her I caused a tremor. It sent a shock wave that raised an army of long-dead sea rogues and villains."

"Okay, let's say that's exactly what happened. What went wrong, Stanley? Where is the Ibis now?" said Mrs. Carelli.

"She sits in the belly of the pike, who now swims in the lake out on the moor. The dear old pike knew the Ibis should not touch the water and that if she did, all the long-forgotten spirits of the evil pirate world would awaken. There is a name for it. It is what they call the Quickening.

"You see, Daisy and I were trying to hide the pike from the first batch of rogues and so I had strapped the pike across my back. But as we walked across the moor I slipped and the pike ended up in the water. And now we sit in wait for the grim and the gruesome."

"Stanley, it all sounds more than ridiculous, you must admit," insisted Mrs. Carelli.

"I know it docs, but the pike has never lied to me or warned me of anything that didn't happen."

"What on earth do you mean, lied to you?"

"Mrs. Carelli, the pike speaks. In a strange tongue but nonetheless, he very definitely speaks!" Stanley persisted.

"Well, that's the daftest load of old hogwash I ever did hear. A talking pike! He never said anything to me, and I dusted him down a million times. The sooner you get ghostly pirates out o' your head, the better. I said you wasn't well and I know I'm right. You need a good night's sleep, lad. And before you get any ideas, young man, I think your precious little Ibis is better off left where it is for now. Out o' sight and away from here."

Stanley turned up his nose at the thought. He was determined to retrieve the pike and the Ibis as soon as possible.

There was a knock on the window. The top of a face appeared, and a hand waved at them.

"That looks like Daisy from the lighthouse, Stanley," sighed Mrs. Carelli. "Come in, poppet," she shouted through the glass. "Door's open."

Daisy's fresh-faced entrance brought light into the room and just naturally eased the argument.

"I brought fish from Uncle Lionel," Daisy announced.

Stanley lifted the cloth from

Daisy's basket, and as he did, a live fish jumped into the air and slapped him on the face.

"Ouch!"

"Ha! Saves me doing it," said Mrs. Carelli as she wandered off into the kitchen.

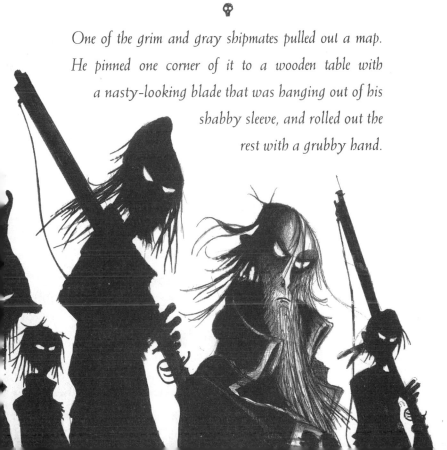

One of the grim and gray shipmates pulled out a map. He pinned one corner of it to a wooden table with a nasty-looking blade that was hanging out of his shabby sleeve, and rolled out the rest with a grubby hand.

Another man stood behind him, peering over his shoulder at the greens and blues of the map. Taking a long knife from his inside pocket, he dropped it on a small olive-colored shape in the southwesterly corner. It stuck in firmly, the blade swaying from side to side.

"That's where we wants to be, sir."

"Fanking you kindly," came a sneering reply. "Best get goin', then. Hoist the mainsail, you dirty, stinkin' old sea dogs."

While Stanley lay sleeping in his bed that night, the creaking wooden shape of a rotting ship moved stealthily through the night. Its ragged black sails flapped violently in the wind, and a band of grisly shipmates drank to their own good fortunes down below.

Soon there would be more. From far and wide they had begun to assemble; some came in groups, some alone. All heading for the same remote corner of the earth.

Beyond the Bronze Warrior

Stanley lay comfortably wrapped up in the warmth of his bed. He had drifted off into a deep sleep, with a candle still flickering by his bedside. The faint light illuminated his face in the darkness until it finally petered out.

Stanley began to dream. In the dream he swam effortlessly through the lake out on the moor. Deeper and deeper he went, until there

was nothing around him but a bottomless black.

Staring eyes and sharpened teeth soared up toward him from the abyss. It startled him before he realized it was his old friend the pike.

Circling Stanley's head and drifting effortlessly around him, the pike began to speak.

"Help me, Stanley. It is time for me to return. Do not blame yourself for what happened; it was a mere accident. You are sitting in wait for the full force of the Quickening to materialize, and I fear that down here, I cannot help you. Take me home, Stanley. The Ibis sits in my stomach, and her heart beats so hard that it gives me a bellyache. I long for my place on the wall. I had grown to love my glass case, but I did not realize it until I was outside it. I fear I am growing old, and though at one time the cold did not bother me, now it bites at my bones and I long for the warmth of the house."

Suddenly Stanley felt the urge to reach the surface. He soared quickly upward, desperate to grab a breath of air. As he burst through, he woke with a start.

He sat up wide-eyed in his bed, peering into the gloom.

"Just a dream," he said, lying down again.

But the dream would not leave him alone. It repeated itself all night and woke him endlessly, until the morning light pierced through the tiny hole in the heavy curtains.

A rotted flag waved through the mist. Grim voices bellowed through the darkness.

A crash of waves broke across the quarterdeck and drenched the ghastly crew.

Down in the cabin, three poisoned-looking faces sat together at a large wooden table, spilling grog across the maps.

A rogue, tattooed from head to toe, raised his tankard.

"I swear that as long as my rotten spirit wanders this earth, I, Scribbles Flanaghan, will seek out the Ibis and bring it 'ome to its rightful place, 'ere on board the Rusty Blade. And if we 'appen to spy the silver casket on our travels, well, that is ours also. Do you swear by the same, Mister Smiff?" he asked his nearest partner.

"That I do, Mister Scribbles, sir. That I do," said Seafood Smith. He popped another crab claw open and swallowed it down with a swig of ale.

"And what about yerself there, Mister Doyle? Will yer be saying the same?"

"You can count on Doyle, me hearties. I will fight to the end to take back what once was mine." He pulled a pair of nasty-looking pliers from his top pocket. "I always 'as a little trick up me sleeve to get what I want. They don't call me Doyle the Dentist for nothin'," he sneered as he opened and closed his pincers. They all laughed out loud.

Someone rattled down the staircase from up on

21

deck, spluttering and gasping and soaked in sea wash. "Mister Scribbles, sir, permission to speak, sir."

"Out with it, Mister Phipps. What is troubling you?"

"There's another ship, sir. A pirate ship, sir, up ahead. She looks like getting there afore us."

"Well get a move on then, Phipps, and stop blubberin'." Scribbles raised his voice and sent a grog bottle hurtling at the back of Phipps's head. "The Rusty Blade will not be beaten by any other ship."

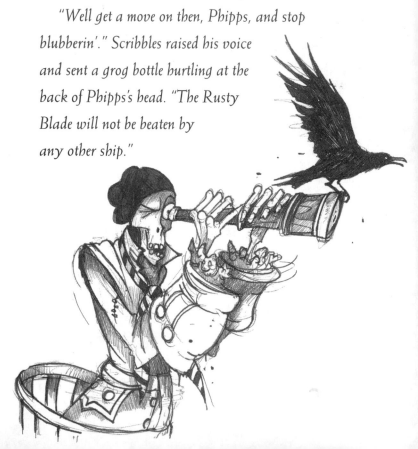

Stanley had drifted off again. He was rudely awakened by the sound of someone rapping at the front door. He listened for Mrs. Carelli and, sure enough, her footsteps clomped across the polished floor of the hallway.

"Hello, poppet," he heard her say. He knew it was Daisy—Mrs. Carelli used that name for her and for nobody else.

In the short time that Stanley had known Daisy, they had become firm friends, and already they had been through thick and thin together. It was a short walk from Daisy's uncle's lighthouse to the Hall, and she spent much of her time at Stanley's side.

Stanley gathered himself together and thundered down the staircase, desperate to tell Daisy about his dream. But only when Mrs. Carelli was out of the way.

He waited for his moment and then he pounced. It was strange to retell the story in daylight.

"But it's only a dream, Stanley," Daisy reassured him. "It doesn't really mean anything."

"Daisy, listen. We can't leave the Ibis where it is. It is vulnerable, and if we have it, we can protect it. If we leave it in the water, they will come and take it easily, without any challenge. The dream is a warning. We must act."

"All right, then. When?"

"Soon. But when we return with the pike we'll have to hide him. Mrs. Carelli won't be happy if she knows that he is back here, with the Ibis in his belly. We need a hiding place, somewhere that doesn't get cleaned regularly. But that rules out most of the house!"

"It is time for me to show you something," announced Daisy. "I haven't gotten around to telling you about this, but now the time is right."

Looking at her, Stanley narrowed his eyes. "The time is right for what?"

Daisy took him by the hand and led him through the maze of winding corridors of the ground floor, past the pictures encased in huge wooden frames and the strange objects in cabinets.

Stanley was intrigued. Even now, Daisy still knew the old place better than he did. When she used to clean for Mrs. Carelli, she had come to know every nook and cranny there was to find.

Finally they stood at the end of a corridor, facing the figure of an ancient warrior cast in bronze.

"What do you think, Stanley?"

"What do I think? Well, yes, it's very

impressive but . . . I've seen it before. I've been here long enough to know it was there. Daisy, what has this got to do with anything?"

She giggled to herself. "You really have no idea, do you?"

The figure held a broadsword in its hand. Daisy gripped the sword's handle and pulled on it, making a satisfying clunk. Then she grabbed the front of the figure and heaved at it.

It suddenly became obvious to Stanley that the ancient warrior was also a huge door.

"Help me, then!" Daisy asked.

Stanley was mesmerized and didn't move for a moment.

"It's amazing what you find by accident when you're dusting," Daisy said as Stanley gathered himself together and helped her to pull the heavy casing wide open.

A blast of cold air rushed out at him from inside. He couldn't see what was up

ahead, but it
appeared to be some
kind of tunnel.

"Where does it go?"
he asked, grinning from ear to ear.

"Why don't you find out?" said Daisy, smiling. "You'll need a light'"

Stanley ran to his room and returned, clattering down the steps, with the small candle-holder that had been placed by his bed.

"What you up to, young Buggles?" came a voice from upstairs.

"Nothing, Mrs. C-C-Carelli, I promise." And he disappeared too quickly for her to ask questions.

In a moment Stanley was winding his way into the darkness with Daisy clutching his shoulder. The way ahead was black and narrow. Their heads were near the roof of the tunnel, and they had to bend slightly to save themselves from getting bumped.

The passage seemed to be never-ending, turning and twisting. All the while Daisy hung on behind Stanley and urged him onward.

Just when Stanley thought it would never stop, the path began to open up. He thought he could hear the rush of the sea in the distance. "Go on," Daisy said. "You're nearly there."

Soon they were standing in a huge cave where the sea came in to form a large pool. A circular opening led out to where the water crashed against the rocks on the south side of the island. Bits of driftwood swam in the foamy water that spilled over the limestone. All around them were craggy platforms and hiding places. An old cupboard lay lopsided against a wall of rock, and a little wooden rowboat was tied to a stone pillar.

"I love it!" cried Stanley as he turned to Daisy. She could hardly hear him. The wind whistled through the cave's opening, and the crash of the surf almost drowned out his voice.

"Why the cupboard?" he asked.

Daisy shrugged her shoulders and held her hands aloft. "Don't know!"

"Why didn't you tell me before?" he shouted through the thunder of the water.

"Well, I've hardly had the time," she answered. "We've both been more than busy since we met!" She came closer so that she could be heard more easily. "Stanley, we should get back. Mrs. Carelli will be suspicious."

"Does she know about this place?"

"No, but she will if we don't get a move on. We can return when we need to. Come on!"

Stanley looked at his candle. The gust had wiped out its flame.

"Prepare yourself, Daisy," he announced. "We'll have to make our way in the dark."

And she held on to the tail of his jacket as they felt their way back through the blinding blackness.

An ancient stone block began to shift, disturbing the
stalks and tendrils that had held it fast for a thousand
years. Hordes of spiny black insects were startled into
movement in every direction.

A skeletal hand with brittle, blackened nails curled
itself around the crumbling slab and forced a meager
opening. Two narrowed eyes peered out from the black
pit. And then, snakelike, the bony frame of Angel Cuzco

slithered out from this prison. Dressed in red, he had a shock of white hair, with two odd bumps on his back.

Nearby, an identical stone moved sideways, and out climbed two more figures. They were dreadful to behold, swathed in long coats embedded with silt and sand, stinking and soggy. Long, lank hair hung over their shoulders, and their red, bloodshot eyes struggled in the light that they had not seen for so many years.

"What names do you go by?" asked Angel Cuzco.

"I am Captain Alvaro Villegas and this is my twin brother, Mauricio," said one of the pair.

"I remember you. We fought together along the coast of South America," said Angel. He felt his rusty memory come back to life. "We were the pride of Peru for many years. Everyone feared us. You, Alvaro, were my captain and we were, all of us, like a band of brothers."

The twins stared, their memories coming back too. They remembered the might of Angel Cuzco and how they had been proud to fight for each other like mad men.

"Why did you awaken from your ancient tombs?" asked Angel.

"The same reason that you did," declared Alvaro. "The Ibis is alive, and the silver casket sits in wait for the final piece in the puzzle. Will you join us on the journey from Peru?"

A green glow appeared in Angel's eyes, a fire

35

from within. His passion for the Ibis was strong. Stronger than anybody's, he thought. The Ibis belonged to him and only him.

"No. I shall not join you. I shall go alone, and when I reach the home of the Ibis I will take it for myself and no one and nothing will stop me."

He said no more. And before they could show their surprise, he drew his sword and cut both of them in two.

Their bodies lay slumped at his feet. He grinned the most evil grin, which turned into vicious laughter. It rang out into the air, and even the parrots in the branches above flocked away.

He pulled back the lid of the ancient tomb and threw the brothers' filthy bones back inside.

Only then did he set off. He walked for days until he reached Arequipa and then he headed to the southern coast. When at last he reached the sea, he kept on walking directly into it. There was no boat or ship to take him, but he didn't care. He simply kept on going in the right direction. The water washed around his feet and he felt his weight sink slightly into the sand. Shoals of sea life darted around him.

Soon his submerged body was walking along the seabed. His lank hair floated in back of him, along with his coattails, and his sword was drawn at his side.

On he went through night and day, through the light and dark of shallow and deep waters. As he walked he spoke these words:

"Drive my ancient spirit unto the sacred bird.

Deliver thy casket forged of silver. Prepare for the coming of the Angel, for he walks alone among the dead."

If he had said it a million times, he would surely say it a million times more. Over and over it went. He crushed small bones and fossils beneath his feet as he trod along the cloudy sea bed. His blade swished through the water, and on he marched, farther and farther into the sea.

In Search of the Ibis

Stanley and Daisy were deep in discussion about the Ibis. It was time to get their hands on it, whether Mrs. Carelli liked the idea or not. Perhaps she would be too busy cleaning to notice what they were up to.

"What's the plan then, Stanley?" asked Daisy cheerfully.

"The plan, Daisy, is

that we don't have a plan," he announced.

"Very well," she sighed in an unconcerned fashion, and they set off together over the moor.

The wind was against them and it was harsh out on the hills. Most days you would feel the worst of the weather there, in one of its many forms.

They passed the old water mill and Stanley remembered the rough winter, when they had ventured out together into the blinding snow.

It wasn't long before they were back at the lake. It was calm and serene, save for the wind blowing ripples across the surface and the reeds shaking in the breeze.

Stanley and Daisy stood staring across the

water for some time. They did not really know what they should do about retrieving the pike, but it was peaceful and right now they were happy to sit and enjoy the moment.

Soon the wind dropped and the sun came out.

"We should have brought a picnic, Stanley," laughed Daisy.

"Yes, too bad we are empty-handed," said Stanley.

But at that moment the huge body of the pike leaped up out of the water and landed neatly in his arms. Freezing water drenched Stanley from head to foot and the icy body of the fish chilled him through.

The pike began to speak.

"Ahh, Stanley. I knew in my heart that you would have the good sense to return. Now let us take to the hills, and we can get me home, where the warmth of the Hall awaits me. I have had quite enough of the dark depths of the lake. I don't think I shall be returning, not just yet!"

Stanley and Daisy looked at each other with raised eyebrows.

"Come along, come along. I will catch cold out here in the open air," instructed the pike. "Once you put me in place, we can discuss your next move. There is much to be done."

"Do you still have the Ibis?" questioned Stanley.

"My dear boy, of course I do. Why do you underestimate me so?"

"I wasn't sure I could trust you once you'd entered the water!" Stanley admitted.

"Well in all my watery

days, I have never been so insulted," the pike started—and as the unlikely trio marched across the moor, the argument continued.

Stanley and Daisy weren't sure how to best approach the house with the pike in hand. They decided to slip in through the coal bin at the back of the house and into the kitchen. From there they would sneak across the ground floor and wind their way unseen through the maze of corridors to where the bronze warrior stood in wait for them.

Gingerly, they crept toward the garden gate, taking a good look at the back of the house. All was quiet.

Unbeknownst to them, Mrs. Carelli was staring out of the bedroom window that looked out over the garden.

Something out on the moor caught her eye. She looked up: nothing. Must have been a bird. As she moved to the back of the room, doing this and that, Stanley and Daisy quicky carried the pike across the lawn.

Mrs. Carelli moved back to dust the window. She could hear noises, but by then Stanley and Daisy had clambered through the opening to the coal bin.

"Strange," said Mrs. Carelli to herself. "Young Buggles is up to something, I swear it."

She pressed her face to the window and peered down. But the three were already winding their way carefully through the corridors.

Their feet raced across the floor, and at last Stanley and Daisy reached the lonesome soldier.

Daisy tugged at the handle. It was stuck!

The familiar clang of Mrs. Carelli's brass

dustpan resounded nearby. They looked up in panic. She wasn't there, but she was close.

"Hurry, Daisy, hurry!" pleaded Stanley.

"I'm trying," she panicked.

And then the pike started complaining. "Stanley, where is this? I did not request to be placed in this part of the house."

"Quiet!" insisted Stanley.

"Is that you, Master Buggles?" came a familiar voice.

CLUNK. Daisy did it. But she was forced to pull the heavy door open by herself while Stanley stood with his arms full, feeling frustrated.

The gap was forced wide enough for them to sneak through. Once inside, they pulled it shut, realizing that they were without a light to show the way. Daisy bravely went first, and pulled Stanley along because his arms were full.

"Ridiculous," continued the pike. "It is as cold and dark in here as in the dreary lake. This is a punishment, is it not?"

They felt their way through the darkness.

"Where will we put him?" quizzed Daisy.

"What about the old cupboard?" suggested Stanley.

"Yes. Good," said Daisy. When they finally reached it, Stanley was desperate to be rid of the pike's weight. He hurled it through the door, and it landed with a thud.

"This is nothing short of bullying and abuse!" persisted the pike. "I was not aware I would lose my status in the house simply because I've been away a short while. How can I be an adviser from here? Ridiculous!"

In the midst of the waves of protest, they closed the door on the ill-tempered pike. But his voice resounded through the casing of the cupboard. What if it echoed through the cave and was heard in the house?

Stanley gritted his teeth. "Please bear with us. We cannot let Mrs. Carelli know we've rescued you. It's either here or the lake, I'm afraid."

Stanley knew that would shut him up and sure enough, the pike was absolutely silent. Stanley had great respect for the pike, but there were times when he had all the qualities of a badly behaved dog.

They closed the bronze door on the dear old pike and headed back into the hallway.

"That's sorted out then," smiled Stanley, turning to Daisy, who was staring over his shoulder. Mrs. Carelli was standing behind him, peering at the two of them, with one eyebrow raised.

"That's what sorted?" she asked. "You're up to something, Stanley. Something sinister. I do hope it's not one o' your crazy plans."

The Legend of Angel Cuzco

Much later, Stanley was in his favorite room, which was full of drawers that held interesting contents. He searched through the piles of books and papers, trying to find something to stop the coming of the ghostly villains who were headed their way. Was there anything he and Daisy could say or do that would be of assistance?

He had searched all afternoon and not found much, but one scrappy piece of old parchment caught his attention. It was a letter. The top part was missing, but beneath it was clear.

An icy chill took hold of Stanley as he read it, and he decided he needed to find Daisy. The letter was something to be shared.

Stanley ran down the stairs shouting Daisy's name. She was in the scullery, leafing through a book.

Stanley sat down at Daisy's side, placing himself in a tall wing-backed chair near the fireplace.

"The first part is missing, Daisy, but listen to this."

Do you know who comes to find you? Have you seen their deadly figures, their ragged bones, and stinking foul faces? They belong to nightmares. To tales of woe and terror.

Do you know of the legend of Angel Cuzco?

Stanley stopped, and he and Daisy looked at each other. The two of them huddled together around the fire and Stanley continued.

Angel was the scourge of the South American coast. Often he joined forces with others, but he was known to like his own company and he feared no one. Dressed in scarlet, with plaited golden-white hair and nut-brown skin, he was a sight, to be sure.

It was maybe two hundred years ago that the Ibis sat buried in a church in Cuzco. It

rested under a stone slab
of a tomb adorned
with the statue
of an angel.

They say the power of the Ibis was so strong that the body returned to life in the form of the angel and stole away with the sacred bird. In a bid to keep it, the angel donned the robes of the pirate trade and fled to the east. He fought so hard to keep it that he became the most feared buccaneer of the seven seas.

He lost the Ibis when he was overcome by a ship carrying monstrous buccaneers.

It is said that his evil ways reduced his wings to stumps upon his back, and that in the end he died defending a gang of Peruvian brothers that he had befriended.

If I were you, I would gather my belongings and escape while there is still a chance that I shall see you again.

Make haste.

Your affectionate brother,

And the rest was torn away.

"Is that a true story, Stanley?" asked Daisy, who, even though sitting by the roaring fire, was shaking like a leaf.

"Well, maybe it is and maybe it isn't. But I'm sure that sooner or later, we will find out." With nervous hands Stanley folded it back into its age-old creases and returned it to the drawer.

The Timber Trail

That night, Stanley and Daisy looked out at the darkness of the ocean from the staircase window. A huge boat had arrived in the harbor.

"They're here," panicked Stanley. The pair of them peered more intently through the glass, squinting their eyes.

"That's no pirate ship, Stanley. It's a ferry!" claimed Daisy.

The two of them stood watching.

Then there was movement. Something began to move down the gangplanks at one end of the boat. The fire baskets were burning, and they illuminated a long winding shape that snaked upward into the harbor, moving toward the moor. It was creaking and grinding like the train that had brought Stanley to the island. What was it?

Stanley and Daisy looked more closely still, and soon they realized that a trail of wooden wagons, one behind another, was approaching them. Flickering lamps hung from them, dancing in the dark.

They ran from room to room, chasing the trail from window to window.

"Wait, I know these people! Don't worry, Stanley," said Daisy. They are travelers, and they have been here before. They are good people, with many friends on Crampton Rock. They will be welcomed. They stay up on the moor when they are here, but recently the curse of the werewolf had driven them away, because many were lost in its grip. They must know the beast is gone—they say that word spreads fast in the world of the traveling man."

On they went to the moor, and when the travelers were far enough out, they rested in a large circle. The light from a campfire laid an orange cast across the hill, and the howl of dogs sailed eerily through the night air. A tent was pitched and sat comfortably protected by the wagons. Silhouettes of people moved around in the warm glow.

The fire danced all night, and Stanley fell asleep to the distant sounds of laughing and singing.

In the morning Stanley was sitting by the fire with a warm drink when a knock at the door disturbed the moment. A tall gypsy man stood in the early light. He had long hair and wore clogs. A heavy coat hung from his shoulders, tied around the waist with rope.

"I come to thank the good lady for the fresh water when we arrived," he chirped. He had an accent that was strange to Stanley, and his manner was pleasant. He pulled his coat open to show a brace of rabbits, and handed them to Stanley.

"Oh . . . er, thank you!" said Stanley.

59

"You must be the lad," the man added. "I wanted to see you."

"Oh! About what?" Stanley quizzed.

"You misunderstand me, son," he said. "I mean, I wanted to see what you look like."

Stanley looked confused. Daisy joined him at the door and they glanced at each other with raised eyebrows.

"The name's Phinn. The folks would like to see you," the man said, confusing Stanley further. "So when you're ready, come along."

And he clomped down the path in his clogged feet and walked back across the moor.

Mrs. Carelli was behind Stanley now. She placed warm hands across his shoulders.

"Don't worry, Stanley. They are good people. They were the first ones on the island, and they gave this place to us. Sometimes they are here for months, and sometimes only days. But this time they come for you. Among other things they bring help and they bring hope. We may have a fight on our hands, but all is not lost. Not yet."

They looked out to sea and wondered what would next appear over the horizon.

"The pirates are coming," said Stanley. "And we cannot keep them at bay forever."

"Go and see the travelers, Stanley. They may hold the answer to our problems," suggested Mrs. Carelli.

Stanley went to get himself ready. In half an hour he would be climbing up to the moor.

7

the Glass Ball

"Will you come with me, Daisy?" asked Stanley, wrapping his coat around him.

"Of course," she replied, and they made their way out of the kitchen door and across the back lawn to the rusted gate. They trod the beaten track on to the moor, where the home of the travelers spread out before them.

As they drew near they could see that there were more tents pitched around the central one and that the fire was still burning. Small children ran in and out of the wagons, and lank dogs with missing legs meandered aimlessly around the camp.

Stanley remembered his first encounters with the dogs of Crampton Rock: all of them with lost limbs, and all of them escaped victims of the werewolf. Here was a sure sign that the travelers were no strangers to this peculiar island.

A group of people were standing around in a ring, and in the middle two giant men were boxing each other bravely with bare hands.

It was strange to see so much activity out on the moor.

But when Stanley and Daisy came close, everything stopped. People turned and looked, putting down their tools or whatever they were holding. The children stopped playing and the boxers lowered their fists.

They all came forward and held out their hands to Stanley. Phinn appeared again. He stood on a wheel of one of the wagons and addressed everyone.

"This young man is Stanley Buggles. He banished the curse of the wolf from these lands, killing the beast that took our brothers and leaving us free to settle here whenever we please."

The crowd cheered and the people shook Stanley's hand and ruffled his hair. One of the boxers picked him up and carried him above his head. They arrived at one of the tents and Phinn followed, bringing Daisy with him.

The boxer placed Stanley back on his feet and held out a giant hand. "My name is Bartley. My brother was taken from me by the wolf, and I wear his memory on my heart. Thank you, boy," he said. "I will be forever grateful to you."

He had the biggest, strongest hands that Stanley had ever seen, yet he seemed as gentle as it was possible to imagine.

Inside the tent, an old woman sat at a small table. A length of fabric was thrown over it, concealing its legs and lower section. On top there was an object covered in a velvet cloth.

Two halves of a barrel were placed at her side to form a pair of seats.

She invited the guests to sit down and be comfortable, and someone brought a strange drink that boiled with smoke. They didn't dare ask what was in it, but they drank it and licked their lips and asked for more.

"My name is Greta," said the old woman. She had a soft, gentle voice and she was old and craggy. "We want to help you, Stanley. You are a friend of the gypsies now, and your enemies are ours also. Give me your hands."

Stanley held them out to her and she clutched them in her own. They were dry and creased, but smooth to touch and much warmer than his. Then she took the velvet cloth away and revealed a glass ball in the middle of the table.

"Lay them on the crystal. It will help," she said, staring hard into the sphere. "Do you see them, Stanley? Do you see what awaits you?"

It meant nothing to Stanley. He could not see anything except for the glass ball with his hands on the top and the old woman gazing into it with her face lighting up in surprise.

"What . . . what is it?" asked Stanley.

"They come from all corners of the earth. And they come in their thousands. From the depths of the ground they stir, like swarms of poisonous insects. Of all the enemies that come, one ship sails alone. When she arrives she will settle in the north bay. She wears the Yellow Jack and none will come near her."

"What does that mean?" Daisy piped up.

"The Yellow Jack is the flag flown in warning of the fever," Greta explained.

"You mean that one of the ships is filled with pirates who are ill?"

"Yes, dreadfully ill. They have the buccaneer's bones, a disease to punish the worst of any pirate spirits. But they will try and get here all the same. The Ibis draws them near."

"We must be extra careful to avoid the sickness then," said Stanley.

"It cannot harm you, Stanley. It is an illness of those who wander the earth in their skeletal form. The spirit is willing, but the body turns putrid and poisonous and burns itself out through a ghastly fever. Foul and stinking is the stench of buccaneer's bones. You will surely know it if you come across it."

"And what about the Ibis? How did you know of it, and that it's here?" asked Stanley.

"The legend is older than all of us. The sacred bird has been to more places than all the travelers here put together, and lived a million lifetimes. Most people know nothing of it and of the ones that do, some are good, some bad. Many think they own it, but very few deserve it.

"Your image came to me in my crystal ball when you defeated the wolf. I watched you out there on the moor, brave and alone. From then on your shape showed itself many times in the crystal and I saw you through the spiraling fog of the glass when you discovered the Ibis.

"Right now what matters is that those villains know the Ibis is here, and they want it. There are many traveling men here, Stanley, tough, hard men who will fight to protect you. But they are up against a tough enemy. Strong is he who fights by the side of his own brother. But unbeatable is the man who walks in the shadow of his own death."

Greta looked into the ball again, her face near the glass.

"Who is this who walks along the ocean floor, dressed in red with a shock of white hair and a cutting blade held at his side? With eyes of green, and stumps upon his back?"

Stanley and Daisy froze. So, Angel Cuzco was more than just a legend.

Greta watched carefully. She described murky, darkened depths where weary pirate bones were reassembling themselves out of their old sea chest. A pair of skeletal companions were dressing their ragged selves, and rusted weapons hung from their hands. A broken padlock lay at their feet and the chest was scattered in splinters upon the murky sand.

But two green eyes shone in the bubbling blue of her ball, and with blinding speed the Angel appeared to be marching toward them. He cut through the pirates without pausing and sent their limbs floating like dead fish until they settled in the sand.

Stanley and Daisy sat silently, their faces pale.

"Enough," Greta said. She knew that what she had seen disturbed Stanley and Daisy, and that if she told them any more she would only frighten them further.

The Black Swarm

In the days that followed, Stanley found himself spending more time with his new-found friends. Bartley watched him shadow box and showed him tricks and techniques as they sparred playfully. The big man would hold out his hands as Stanley hooked and jabbed into his palms.

"You have a good pair of hands, Stanley.

Quick and precise. You may need them sooner than you think."

"I know," said Stanley,"and I will be ready." But he knew in his heart of hearts that no man on earth was strong enough to defeat the evil spirits of the dead, and he was plotting a way to keep the island safe from the deadly crew that moved toward them.

Meanwhile, Daisy was making herself popular bringing fresh fish to the camp.

"Courtesy of Mr. Grouse, from the light-house," she would say, and she'd hand over a box of sea bream or mackerel. Then she'd hang around all day, playing with the dogs and the children, until Stanley had tired of his training with the mighty Bartley.

Two more days had passed and Stanley knew that what was coming in their direction would arrive sooner or later. He knew nothing of how far the pirates had traveled, how long they would take, or which way they would come. But still he knew for sure that eventually they would appear, and his anxiety grew and grew until it gave his stomach a twisting, knotted pain.

The very next morning was bleak and black. It was almost as if the sun had not woken, and a misty fog circled the harbor all day. The whole mood of the island seemed to turn, almost as if it knew what was coming.

Black clouds hung heavily over the sea, rolling and rumbling in a brisk wind.

Then, as night was arriving, something poked through the tops of the misty clouds far in the distance. At first it looked like a flock of crows, flapping on the wind. But no. It moved too slowly and steadily.

"Flags," said Stanley. "They are black pirate flags." And as he said it he knew he was right, and his heart sank into his belly. "There is only one thing to do, Daisy," he said calmly.

"And what is that?" said Daisy, staring into his face. "Aren't you terrified?"

"No, Daisy, I am not. I am prepared. At nightfall, I will take the Ibis and be gone. You must cover for me. The ships are close and I must act soon."

"Let me come with you," she begged.

"No way."

"What makes you think you can handle this more than me?" she said angrily, tucking a playful punch into his belly.

"Ooof. All right," he answered. "If you want to be part of it you can. But it will be the hardest thing you ever did."

And that was that. In that instant it was decided.

Within five minutes they were feeling their way through the blackness of the tunnel.

When he reached the cupboard, Stanley

grabbed the pike hurriedly.

"Dear oh dear, whatever next," began the pike. "I was just beginning to get comfortable."

Daisy climbed into the little wooden boat that had sat in wait for them as it bobbed up and down in the pool of the cave. Stanley handed her the pike and pushed them away from the rocks. When he was soaking wet up to his waist, he jumped in.

"Hold on tight to your slippery friend there, Daisy. We don't want him to end up in the water!" warned Stanley.

"I am sure you are fully aware that I am a freshwater creature," muttered the pike. "I am far too sophisticated to dwell among the dregs of marine life."

"You would get on well with my mother," said Stanley. "It's just a shame you will never make her acquaintance." He began to row with all his might, pushing them out through the narrow opening onto the ocean surf. They were around the other side of the island now, away from the onslaught of piracy.

A full moon was pouring light across the harbor, and the mischievous pair readied themselves in their trusty boat. But Stanley soon found he was no oarsman. He couldn't control the boat, no matter how he tried.

"You take hold of our friend here," said Daisy," and I'll do the rowing. I don't think you've found your sea legs yet," she joked. She took the oars from him and immediately the ride became sure and steady. Stanley watched her rowing: despite the rough water, she made it seem effortless. And for someone quite small she was surprisingly strong.

"Where are we heading?" asked Daisy.

"To the north side of the island,'" said Stanley. "To where the Yellow Jack is heading with its sickly crew."

"Stanley, what on earth are you thinking of? We are supposed to be avoiding them, not joining them!" Daisy panicked. Suddenly the boat was carried along on the crest of a wave, and Daisy fought hard to keep them from crashing against the rocks.

Daisy panted, pulling harder on the oars as the little boat bobbed up and down on the swell.

Then, as they cleared the rocks and came out into the deep, they saw ships heading toward them from the other direction.

"Row, Daisy!" cried Stanley. "Row for your life!"

"I'm trying," she gasped, as the drag of the water yanked at her arms.

Stanley had not planned on a choppy sea. The harbor had seemed relatively calm, but here on the other side of the island they were struggling to steady the boat. White froth rushed up the sides and the splashes of water were icy cold.

Before too long, the shape of Crampton Rock was growing smaller as they steered away from the island and the pirate ships.

Darkness and endless water surrounded the little boat. On board, the two small warriors and their fish headed fearlessly into the unknown.

To the pike, Stanley announced something that he knew would not be popular.

"I'm going to take the Ibis from you," he said.

"I had a feeling this was coming, and I fear that you are making a wrong move, Stanley," the pike returned. "I think perhaps there is a better way.

"I don't think you have a better way," said Stanley. "Firstly, you have no idea what my plan is and secondly, if you do and there is an easier solution I'd like to know what it is."

"I'm thinking!" insisted the pike, and he closed his mouth tightly so that Stanley had no chance of retrieving the Ibis.

"This is no time for games," said Stanley, who felt a growing frustration. "Open wide, please."

But the mouth stayed shut and the eyes glared at him.

"Very well," said Stanley, thinking quickly. "If you refuse to cooperate, then I shall have no option but to place you in the salt water among the sea life."

"Yes, and I hear the tiger sharks are particularly hungry at this time of year," suggested Daisy. She still wasn't entirely sure of Stanley's plan, but nonetheless she was prepared to see it through.

The pike's eyes seemed set even wider as Stanley lifted him up and dangled him by his tail. The Ibis rolled to the front of his mouth and finally he allowed it to drop into the bottom of the boat.

"Thank you," said Stanley. He didn't want to upset the pike, but time was of the essence. He retrieved the Ibis from the boat and slipped it neatly inside a square of cloth.

They rounded a cliff face, and suddenly a blackened shape hung over them. A filthy silhouette of sheer evil swayed on the surf.

Voices bellowed out, and the torn and ragged shapes of sails flapped noisily in the gust.

They had no idea what ghastly contents this vessel would contain. But all three of them knew that they were about to find out.

The Evil Within

Stanley and Daisy were dwarfed by the might of the hulking shape of the ship's silhouette and they huddled tightly beneath it. On board, lamplights twinkled like stars here and there. The ship's name was painted on its side. The Rusty Blade.

Stanley told Daisy to steer right up to the underside of the ship. It wasn't easy, by any means, but somehow she managed it.

"Perfect," said Stanley. "Hang on here." He pulled himself up onto the side of the boat with the aid of the anchor chain that speared downward through the water. He had the Ibis tucked neatly into his inside pocket.

There was no one on deck. That was a stroke of luck. Stanley crept across the boards to the main mast and clambered up toward the yellow flag. Then when he could grasp hold of it, he tore it hastily from the ropes and shoved it inside his shirt.

"Now where on earth are you going?" whispered Daisy as loud as she dared.

"Just making a little delivery," he said, waving the Ibis at her with a spare hand.

Daisy was confused, but she trusted his judgment and knew that if she did her job and kept the boat right there waiting for him,

everything would be all
right.

She sat and watched
him lurch down the
barnacled side of the
rotting ship. He wasn't far
from the water before
he stopped and
dug his hand
into a rotted

hole. He
tore at it fiercely
until it was big

enough for him to sneak through. Bits of splintered wood plopped into the waves.

Daisy cringed, clenching her sweating hands into fists. She did not know what she would do if someone appeared. She watched until the soles of Stanley's shoes were the last thing to drop through the hole.

Inside, Stanley crept around in the dark. He had stumbled into the crew's quarters, and knew that he had to scramble his way down to the stores at the bottom of the ship without being found by any of the spirits that lurked on board.

He felt his way along the slime and grease that seemed to coat the ship's sides. Voices grew nearer. Too near.

Stanley hurried as much as he could. He had decided to place the Ibis in the ballast at the bottom of the ship. Here it would be concealed, and no one would stumble on it. He was sure that we would be able to make it back to the ship to reclaim it when this was all over.

Something opened up to reveal a lower level. He stepped down carefully and felt for the floor beneath him. A layer of cold hard stones. This was it, the ballast. The stones were used as a weight to stabilize the frame of the ship.

In the far corner, he found a memorable spot. Bilge rats scurried over his hands and around his feet as he burrowed his fingers through the hard rugged surface that cut at his knuckles. He buried the Ibis right there, wrapped in its cloth protection.

And then he made his way back through the blackness the way he had come.

"What's that?" asked Scribbles Flanaghan, pricking up an ear, and his dreadful figure stepped into the light of the oil lamp. A cascade of endless tattoos was illuminated in the dark, and his two yellowy eyes opened wider.

"I can 'ear somethin'. Down in the stores. Ain't no one down in the stores, is there? Mister Smiff, will you be so kind as to investigate and while you're at it, take Mister Doyle with yer in case someone needs a reminder that we ain't 'ere to be messed with!"

"Aye, aye, Mister Flanaghan, sir. Seafood Smiff at your service." He got to his feet, swallowing a handful of cockles, and was followed by Doyle into the damp darkness of the hold.

Stanley was still feeling his way back and he cringed as he creaked on the floorboards.

"There's someone 'ere, or that's a huge rat I can 'ear," said Doyle. "And when I get my 'ands on 'em I'm gonna do 'em some damage."

Abruptly and unintentionally, Stanley's outstretched hand landed in Doyle's grizzly face.

"Agghhhh!" They both screamed, but Doyle held on to Stanley's arm and twisted it as he gripped.

"Who goes there? Friend or foe?" said Doyle as he squeezed tightly.

Stanley felt the cold slimy grip of death.

Whatever or whoever it was that held him stunk to high heaven. He held his free hand over his mouth.

"Nothing . . . nobody . . . I mean . . ."

struggled Stanley as he tried to think of the right thing to say. Doyle's gruesome face came closer through the dark. He was holding up a pair of pliers.

"Over 'ere, Mister Smiff," grunted Doyle to his companion. "We got a customer for the dentist's chair."

Stanley really didn't like the sound of that.

The foul-smelling twosome leered at him through the dim light. Their yellowy eyes came far too close.

"It's a boy! An ugly little feller 'e is an' all," exclaimed Doyle. "Shall we kill 'im now?"

"O' course we will," Smith croaked. "We'll do it with this." He shoved a cutlass under Stanley's nose.

Stanley panicked. But he was now only an arm's length from the hole where he had squeezed in. He lunged for the escape route with his free hand and began pulling himself out. Doyle held on to him tightly, but his arm was forced through the hole along with Stanley.

Smith lunged at him through the dark, swinging his blade, but he just kept hacking at the side of the ship. Chips and splinters of rotten wood fell to the floor as he swore in frustration.

Daisy looked up at Stanley in panic; she could see he was in trouble. But before she could act, he was out. He had shoved the weight of his body through the hole, and now he was dropping headlong into the boat. Daisy let out a piercing scream. As Stanley sat up he realized why: Doyle's bony, skeletal arm had ripped out of its socket and had held on to him as he fell into the boat. The fingers were still moving. Stanley ripped it off his shirt and threw it into the water.

"Row, Daisy, row!"
he cried.

Inside, Doyle
and Smith
snarled in
despair, but their
anger was overtaken
by the onset of a
strange sickness. Beads of
black sweat began to form
on their brows.

On the way back Stanley and Daisy did
not speak. They just kept rowing. At one
point Stanley swapped with Daisy to give
her a rest, but he was sloppy and unfocused
and Daisy was forced to resume rowing by
herself.

In the distance, the ships of the Black

Swarm veered to the north side of the island. Somehow they could sense the Ibis, resting in the ballast of the Rusty Blade.

The deadliest villains of the pirate world were about to collide.

"Are you all right, Daisy?" asked Stanley.

"Yeah, I'm fine," she replied. "Just fine. But tell me something. Did that go according to plan, or do I just not understand what's going on?"

"Don't worry. Like I said, it will work. The Ibis is on board the ship, and though she draws the pirates near, she is protected."

"By what?"

"Well, by the illness. Those villains are suffering, Daisy. They smelled awful, and they are on the brink of death. The power of the Ibis will speed up the sickness. All will be drawn to the ship, and all will die," explained Stanley. It was a plan made in heaven. "When they are all gone, we can return and retrieve the Ibis.

☠

Back on board the *Rusty Blade*, it was mayhem. Doyle and Seafood were fighting. Their knives were drawn and they danced around each other warily, stabbing the air.

"Stop this nonsense!" shouted Flanaghan. "What's goin' on?"

"It's 'im," cried Doyle. "I lost me arm and he's laughin' at me!"

"How on earth did you manage that, Doyle? I only asked you two to see what the bloomin' noise was."

And then something distracted Flanaghan. He turned and looked around, holding the lamp up inside the cabin.

"Something's different," he began. "I can feel it."

"Feel what, sir?" asked Doyle.

"The Ibis. It's near. Somehow, closer than it was." Flanaghan wanted to search, but the illness was making all of them sicker. Their skin grew more yellow and their fever boiled harder by the minute. It was only a matter of time before it had them firmly in its grip. They would take the Ibis first if they could, but they were all struggling.

"Tomorrow we will search hard," Flanaghan claimed. "But tonight I need rest." He checked his reflection in a broken bottle and groaned at his weary expression. Then he took to his quarters and fell flat on his bed.

Scarecrow Point

Stanley and Daisy were struggling in the little wooden boat, blown around on the surf. Up ahead a small island loomed, and they were sent crashing onto the rocks that spilled around it.

"We'll have to stop here, Daisy. It's too dangerous to go on."

"No, not here," insisted Daisy. "That's

Scarecrow Point."

"What's wrong with it?" asked Stanley, frustrated.

"Stanley, Scarecrow Point is haunted."

"By what?" Stanley grimaced doubtfully as Daisy pulled frantically on the oars, gasping and wheezing.

"By a scarecrow. What else?" she puffed. "Once these hills were farmed, but then, the story goes, a scarecrow came to life and frightened the workers away. First the scarecrow disappeared, then he was seen waving his arms and screaming at passersby. No one comes here now."

"Personally I have no faith in the supernatural," piped up a voice. It was the pike, who had been listening all along.

"Daisy, I'm sorry. We have little choice," cried Stanley, who did not care much for the tale of the scarecrow but did care more for his own life. "And besides, you need the rest," he insisted. They edged nearer to the rocky shore.

Finally they washed up on to the rocks and clambered out. Daisy held on tight to the pike, and Stanley pulled the boat in to safety so it wouldn't carry itself out to sea. They struggled upward and found solace at the top of the Point, where the trees grew densely and there was good cover.

Stanley and Daisy watched the pirate ships come nearer. It grew dark and cold but they were against the idea of lighting a campfire because it would only draw attention. They sat in fear and panic as the daylight faded fast. Despite Stanley's excellent plan, he felt he had no real way of knowing exactly what would happen.

Suddenly, Daisy saw a skinny, muddy face
with wild, staring eyes appear behind Stanley.
The little figure was dressed in rags and had
untamed hair and a matching beard.

Daisy screamed. Stanley would have done the same, but he was unable to catch his breath and wheezed pathetically instead.

"Children. At last. Where did you spring from? I have not seen anyone in years," came the voice from the figure. It sounded surprisingly gentle, but that didn't stop Stanley and Daisy from jumping to their feet and attempting to escape from the horrifying sight of this scarecrow come to life.

"Calm down, children. Calm down. I am a marooned islander from the Rock, abandoned here by pirates who attacked my boat. I do not intend to harm anyone. I only seek to leave this place."

He was so frail and kind that they immediately believed him, and felt obliged to explain their own intentions.

"We are fleeing from the fleet of ships

heading this way," stammered Stanley.

The straggly man got to his feet and stood staring out to sea at the pirate ships. "In all my days I've never seen nothing like it," he gasped. "You really are in trouble. You need to keep moving. But don't go back to the Rock, not in the darkness. The curse of the wolf awaits you there."

"You have been away a while, sir," said Stanley. "There is no longer any threat from the wolf." He stared at the man they had thought was a scarecrow. "But . . . who are you? How do you know about the wolf?"

"Never mind me, son," said the man. "You can cross the island and continue from there. The water is safer on that side, and you're only a short journey from the Rock. I will help you move your boat and perhaps, on your return, you could get me help?"

They did as the strange man suggested. When Stanley and Daisy had climbed into the vessel, Stanley thanked him. "Maybe it is better if you come with us," suggested Stanley. "Back to the island."

The man looked at the boat. It was tiny. "I think you have a full load already. I wouldn't wish to compromise your circumstances."

"I do not wish to be rude," began Stanley, "but you are neither big nor heavy. I don't think you will make much difference."

And as he spoke, Daisy pushed up and patted the space beside her.

The man held his hands together. "Thank you, children," he said. "I grow too old and weak to look after myself out here. It is cold and unwelcoming, and at night it is as black as can be. Someday, I shall repay you"

"Make yourself comfortable," said Stanley.

"But you must tell us who you are."

As the four of them set sail under the gathering moonlight, the pike fell gently to sleep and the man began his tale.

"I was a simple tradesman. But once while I was out fishing, I was set upon by pirates who wrecked my boat and left me stranded on that island, with only plowed fields and an old scarecrow. I dismantled the scarecrow and put on his clothes, and then I learned to fend for myself. Often I would try to escape or catch the attention of passing ships, but all to no avail."

As Stanley looked at him in the moonlight he saw how his straggly long-haired figure could resemble the shape of some mad scarecrow spirit, dancing around with desperate, flailing arms.

"And what name do you go by?" asked Stanley.

"My name is Victor. Victor Carelli. And I hope that somewhere, my wife still waits for me."

Stanley and Daisy stared at each other in wild surprise. But they did not say anything.

Not yet.

The boat bobbed along on the water and soon they were close to the island. They hit land and began to walk across the moor.

Victor felt good being back on the Rock. He could see the twinkle of candlelight down in the houses, and a flutter of excitement leaped around inside him.

They came to the gypsy camp, and Bartley

appeared through the darkness.

"Come to the tents!" he shouted.

The travelers greeted Victor with open arms. He had many old friends here. They had known of his disappearance and now they rejoiced at his return. Someone wrapped a blanket around him and sat him by the fire. Someone else brought him hot broth, and everyone gathered around, staring at his wild appearance in astonishment touched with amusement.

But inside the main tent, Greta was waiting for the children, ready to warn and ready them for a surprise.

"Prepare yourself, Stanley." Greta said. "They draw near, but we are right behind you. In the meantime there is something else. I know you keep secrets well, but do you have room in your heart for another?"

"I suppose so," Stanley said, with uncertainty.

"And you, Daisy. Can you be faithful to your friend here and protect a lamb from the prying eyes of wolves?" Greta asked.

"Of course," said Daisy, equally perplexed.

"Then pull back the velvet fringe that runs around the bottom of the table, my dear, and tell me what you see," she requested.

Daisy did as she was asked, and before their eyes lay the beautifully crafted shape of a silver casket. Lost for thousands of years, and seen by only a few.

It took Stanley's breath away and he felt a rush of blood to the head. He was looking at something he thought he would not see in his lifetime. Something that had been described to him by his Great Uncle, Admiral Swift and that he felt privileged just to look upon.

"Now you know why the gypsies came, Stanley," murmured Greta. "We came to thank you for what you gave to us. The freedom to return to Crampton Rock. What you see before you is yours," explained Greta gently. She urged them to look more closely at it.

The casket looked perfect, forged so beautifully and intricately in shining silver that seemed to echo every other color when the light was on it, just like the Ibis.

Its shape was rectangular and the lid rounded like an old pirate's chest. It had little short legs and they too were intricately formed but every bit of it was unique. It was smaller than Stanley had expected.

But when they examined it in detail, they could see that something was missing.

Stanley looked at the sections of the lock. It was just as Admiral Swift had described it last summer: a Jackal and a Bison, and then a space where the missing Ibis fitted.

At first he did not dare touch the casket, but then he could not resist. It was heavy. Perhaps something inside was making it so? He wouldn't know what it was until he placed the Ibis in the lock and opened the lid.

"The silver casket has carried many secrets over the years, Stanley. What it hides now, I cannot say. Something important, I am sure," said Greta. "Take it home, and when the time is right you can open it there."

"You must examine its contents in secrecy," said Bartley, who was standing next to Stanley. "It is yours now, and a private matter between you and the casket."

Bartley escorted Stanley, Daisy, and Victor as far as the long path that led to the house, and waited until they were safely inside.

In a flash, before they did anything else, they hid the casket in Stanley's room. It would have to wait there until, he hoped, he would again get his hands on the Ibis and have a chance to open the casket with it. They put the pike away again in his cupboard.

Once they were done, they sat Victor in the kitchen, preparing him to meet the housekeeper of Candlestick Hall.

"Listen, Victor," began Daisy. "There is a lady who works here, and she will be interested to see you. She will arrive shortly, and will probably be looking for us, and will be angry, I'm sure—but I feel you may change her mood."

And with that, Mrs. Carelli came bursting through the door. She had been out, desperately searching for Stanley and Daisy.

"Stanley Buggles, where have you b—? Who is thi—?"

Victor stood up. He looked wearily at the woman he had married, and who he'd thought he would never see again. "Violet . . .

it's me," he said, and his eyes filled up uncontrollably. "I'm back." His voice wobbled and tears left clean streaks across his muddy face.

"Oh Victor, my goodness." Mrs. Carelli held her hands up to her mouth, and for a second she looked as if she was about to drop to the floor. But then she ran forward and grabbed him close in her arms. His tiny figure bent like a rag doll as she held on to him tight.

"Is this the moment where we disappear?" suggested Daisy.

"Ahh . . . yes," agreed Stanley, and they slipped out of the room.

They headed upstairs to stare at the casket again, and went to the window to look at the boats.

It looked as if Stanley's plan was working. The endless fleet was heading north, to the small bay where the Rusty Blade drew them near.

Stanley turned to Daisy. They shook hands and grinned happily.

A few hours later, Victor was sitting on a tall stool in the kitchen, and Daisy was making use of her hairdressing skills to tidy him up. Mrs. Carelli looked on in admiration as Daisy trimmed off clumps of hair, which fell to the floor, and she saw the face of the man she knew reappear before her.

His face was drawn and thin, and he had what Stanley's mother called a weather tan, the look of someone who worked outside.

When the beard began to come off, Victor felt at his smooth face. It had been years since he had run his hands across his chin. Mrs. Carelli began to cry when she saw his face revealed.

"Oh Violet, please!" said Victor. "Don't start me off again!"

"I still can't believe it," she wept. "I had this awful feeling that when we shaved your hair off we'd find out it was somebody else under there. But it's really you," she blubbered.

They all laughed. Stanley momentarily forgot his troubles as he and Daisy helped to comfort Mrs. Carelli.

But he knew there was work to do and that they should really be readying themselves for . . . well, for anything. The best place for them to be was out on the moor and the best company for them to be in was with the

travelers. Stanley signaled to Daisy, and the
two of them left Mr. and Mrs. Carelli at the
house and headed for the hills.

12

The Coming of the Angel

There was to be no sleep that night on board the Rusty Blade. Nor would there be sleep on any other pirate vessel. The ships were now heading frantically toward the north side of the island where the Rusty Blade was lying, its Yellow Jack now missing that young Buggles had removed it to put his plan into place. Of course, no one who rushed toward it could have predicted that on board a deadly disease awaited. As the Ibis lay sleepily in its hiding place, its presence made the fever boil.

Stanley and Daisy were now making toward the gypsy camp. The campfire glowed in the darkness and they scrambled across the moor toward the orange light.

Greta sat waiting for them. She had seen them coming through the crystal ball.

Bartley greeted them first. "It is good to see you both. You are most welcome," he said. "We are readying ourselves in case we are needed."

Stanley saw that the travelers were making weapons, practicing the art of swordsmanship and close combat. He felt heartened by the fact that he wasn't the only one preparing.

"Quickly, now. Come and see what is happening," beckoned Greta.

She ran her hands over her crystal ball and looked hard through the whirling white mist.

"Look how they fight among themselves," she grinned. Stanley and Daisy could see nothing in the glass ball, and so they were forced to hang on Greta's every word.

"All the ships are closing in on the Rusty Blade. The Ibis draws them near. As they close in, the pirates are growing desperate to reach the Ibis. Not only are the ships attacking those around them, the shipmates are also turning on one another.

"This is indeed a plan made in heaven, children, and I watched you put it into place. Well done. You are braver than most," Greta said warmly.

"I couldn't have done it if you hadn't explained the purpose of the Yellow Jack," said Stanley, smiling.

Drinks arrived, and they sat in comfort for a while. Finally, Stanley and Daisy decided that they must return to the Hall to get some sleep.

The seabed changed beneath the feet of Angel Cuzco. It went from fine white sand to rocks here and there, and then suddenly it was nothing but pebbles and fine shale. Up ahead the water grew shallow, and eventually the golden-white mane of hair that hung from his skull showed itself on the surface. His emerald

green eyes stared out from the shallow surf, and he kept on marching at the same pace until his soaking-wet skeletal form had emerged fully from the ocean waves.

☠

After Stanley and Daisy had left, Greta saw something in the glass ball that would have forced her to keep the children in the camp.

She saw the deathly figure of Angel Cuzco. He was walking across the harbor of Crampton Rock, heading for the moor. His emerald eyes grew greener, for he felt the Ibis so strongly he would have sworn it beat like a heart inside him.

His passion for the Ibis turned into anger as he drew closer. If anything had stood in his way, he would have torn it to pieces.

Greta called for Bartley and Phinn to run and guard the children.

Stanley and Daisy were still making their way across the moor, unaware of this. Up ahead, two small green lights were approaching across the plain. Stanley thought of all sorts of things it could be. A werewolf. The pirates. It could be anything . . . but as they drew nearer they saw a scarlet-coated, white-haired shape descending on them.

Bartley was running up behind. "Stop!" he cried.

It was too late. Angel Cuzco was right before them.

But the children were nothing to him. He simply walked right through them. As he did so, a force knocked them to the ground, leaving them breathless.

Bartley and Phinn showed their battle-worn hands and prepared for the scarlet phantom. The Angel swiped at Bartley with his sword, and using the elbow of the same arm he forced a blow under Phinn's chin. Phinn dropped to the floor but stood straight back up again. Bartley placed a hard right hand into Cuzco's ribs and the bones smashed into pieces. But the spirit had a distinct advantage: he felt no pain.

Stanley and Daisy by now had gotten back on their feet and they joined in. Daisy jumped on Angel's back and yanked his hair. Stanley threw a battery of punches but none of them landed anywhere near Angel.

Then Cuzco dropped his sword and, using both hands with supernatural speed, he grabbed Phinn and Bartley by the hair and pulled their heads together. Crack. They fell to the ground.

Cuzco picked up his blade and tucked it into his belt. Then he turned to the Stanley and Daisy.

"When I return from the ships I will hang you urchins from the gallows," he promised. The Angel grinned a sickly smile and marched toward the north bay. Back inside Greta watched the progress of the Angel in her glass ball but now it clouded over. The whirling mist became a green fog, and she could see nothing.

The gypsy encampment was in a frenzy. They headed to the bay, not knowing what they would find.

The North Bay Battle

The Rusty Blade was surrounded. You could not have counted the number of black silhouettes of sails and flags that swayed in the wind, whirling in circles around the bay. Screaming and shouting filled the air. As the ships neared one another, cannonballs began hurtling through the darkness and clouds of gunpowder popped here and there in the night.

"Drive my ancient spirit unto the sacred bird. Deliver thy casket forged of silver. Prepare for the coming of the Angel, for he walks alone among the dead," he recited to himself. Cuzco watched from the cliff top as the fleet descended on the Rusty Blade.

Some pirates jumped from their ships into the water and climbed up the sides. Others climbed across the rigging of their own ships and jumped down on to the deck. Many sat back and simply fired everything they had at everybody else. It was pure mayhem.

But on board the Rusty Blade, no one made any effort to defend the ship. No one moved at all. Scribbles Flanaghan, one of the deadliest pirates ever to sail the salty waters, lay face down on the floor, loosely holding his last-ever drink of grog. Young Master Phipps had retired to his bed, never to make it out of his bedclothes again. Seafood Smith was slumped over a table with a plate of tentacles and seaweed sauce spilled down his shirt. And Doyle the Dentist, whose torturous treatment was the scourge of the seven seas, lay on his back with his best pair of pliers by his side.

Every one of the gruesome crew was dead, with yellow skin and slimy boils about their bodies. Their green tongues hung out like slabs of rancid meat and their eyeballs had turned black.

And now, the rest of the pirate fraternity climbed on board—unknowingly about to encounter the deadly infection that burned at a thundering pace.

Out on the upper deck, the clash of phantom pirate enemies had begun. They swung awkwardly at each other with cudgels and blades and cursed each one another's names.

Very quickly their bodies became listless and weary. They were drawn to the Ibis, every one, but as they came near they were caught in Stanley's effortless trap. The fever boiled on their brows and the energy of the ancient Ibis spiraled it into a furious force.

There were hundreds of pirates, but soon their grubby corpses lay scattered across the decks. Some had died from the fever and some from the battle. And yet still more came.

Angel Cuzco appeared as if from nowhere. His long white hair and scarlet coat glowed in the darkness, and the lights of his emerald green eyes were enough to frighten the fiercest of men. He was forced into terrifying battle.

Stanley and Daisy had joined back up with the gypsies, and now the full force of the Crampton army stood in silhouette along the cliff top. They watched the north bay battle from the safety of the hills.

Through the stinking, filthy, darkness, the pirates battled and searched for the treasure all night.

After hours of vicious pandemonium the pirates who were left grew distracted from the fight, drawn by the Ibis. Still they sweated at the brow and felt the slimy boils pop up on their skin. They did not notice the illness that grew upon them. They found themselves almost hypnotized by the Ibis, as each and every one of them searched among the stones that lined the bottom of the Rusty Blade.

All except for Angel Cuzco, who stood staring hard at the pebbles, almost as if he could see right through them and then when

he found the spot he would walk right over
to it.

And that's exactly what
he did.

He was strong, stronger
than most. He did not feel
a fever or a shaking
in his limbs.

Stomping his
way through the
crowd of sickly
pirates, he sank his
hand deep down
to where
Stanley had laid
the Ibis. He wrapped
his bony joints around it and plucked it from
its nest.

Then, without a moment's thought, he

stood up straight and climbed to the upper deck. The pirates that still littered the ship were on their knees. The fever was taking their lives quickly, and as they lay upon the deck their gruesome features rotted and only their stinking bones were left. It grew quiet as the noise of gunfire and the screams of war were banished by the silent grip of death.

The ships lay battered and broken on the rocks, and soon the evidence of their presence would be swallowed by the gulf waters.

The Pirate Wolves

But Angel Cuzco was not done. He was strong and he was hungry, and he had not come this far only to suffer illness.

He walked around the deck in the early morning light, picking his way through the bones. He kept the heads of those he knew belonged to the hardest of pirate captains, holding them by their hair: those he had fought in the past and those he had struggled to beat that very night.

With his arms full and his sword tucked by his side, Angel Cuzco headed for the gypsy encampment.

"Put the children in the wagons!" someone cried out. But Stanley and Daisy avoided being rounded up and mingled with the warriors.

The travelers were preparing for the on-slaught. Weapons appeared and the horses were brought forward. Bartley and Phinn, stripped to the waist, held their fists high.

A huge crowd of troops stood in wait: some on horseback, some on foot, many with weapons and many with hardened fists that knew their trade.

The crazy stare of Angel Cuzco came close. Now he wanted the silver casket, and he wanted it desperately. The gypsies could see that he was alone, but that he carried something in his hands.

Inside her tent, Greta had been looking into her ball. She cried out in panic when she saw familiar eyes peering back at her.

"Wolves!" she cried. "I thought we were free of the wolves. Why do they show themselves in the glass?"

Before she could see clearly, but now the green mist came again and choked the picture in the ball. Outside Angel Cuzco stood before the crowd.

The travelers' army looked strong. They would be a handful even for the Angel, and especially since he stood alone.

Angel Cuzco scattered the skulls around him, then began to whisper his words once more.

"Deliver thy casket forged of silver. Prepare for the coming of the Angel, for he walks alone among the dead."

He took his sword and split each skull down its middle. From each shattered head emerged a black shape. At first it was not clear what had materialized, but after only moments, a huge pack of wolves stood at the side of Angel Cuzco. Grisly, slavering, hungry, filthy wolves.

If anything was sure to frighten the travelers, it was the sight of wolves. They had already suffered too much at their mercy of these animals.

But bravery welled up inside them and they stood together. Bartley took a long look. Before him were the same kind of beasts that had taken his brother. His anger pushed back any fear deep down into his stomach, and he stood tall at the front of his army.

Suddenly the encounter began. The beasts lurched forward and darted speedily in the direction of their enemy, and the travelers fought back with fists and cudgels. The horses circled and pushed the wolves back, but they bit awkwardly at their heels and the first blood was drawn.

Cuzco danced around with his arms whipping up a storm as he slashed his blade through the air.

Bartley and Phinn held him off with poles of wood and shields made from barrel tops. But the wolves snaked in around anyone who came close and snapped at them: it was impossible. The dogs reacted, barking with bared teeth, but they were anxious against the might of the black wolves.

As the mist in Greta's ball drew away, something else came clear. Faces. Evil, yellow-eyed faces with shining blades held fast between their rotting teeth. Where did they come from?

Latecomers! The very last of the ghostly pirate ships. Three of them, all filled with sea scoundrels of one kind and another. None of them had caught the fever of the Rusty Blade. Instead, they were heading for the excitement out on the moor, where they grasped a vague sniff of the Ibis.

They scrabbled their way on to the cliffs over rocks and boulders. Daisy noticed them first. She hurled rocks at them and forced them back for a moment. Somehow they made it through, and now the Crampton army was surrounded.

Whether Daisy and Stanley liked it or not, they were in the middle of the fight. Every so often someone would pull them back and push them to one side, but they were not the kind of children to stand and watch. Besides, it was not the first time they had been eye to eye with the full force of the supernatural.

Cuzco moved so fast it was hard to see him. His long white hair flew about his head as he turned and twisted, thrusting wounds here and there. By now, several travelers had been injured, but they pushed on bravely.

Stanley was worried. Perhaps the spirit

of Cuzco could not be defeated no matter what.

The screams and shouts of battle rose up. The crunch of clogs on bones, the thwack of poles and sticks, the whoosh and swipe of the blade, and the cries and screams of pure pain rang out.

Stanley remembered all the moves that Bartley had shown him: throwing punches then moving swiftly out of danger, staying on his toes so he could nimbly step back or forward. Daisy had watched him often, and she followed his lead. They used their fast moves on the new arrivals, and when they had them confused and distracted, the dogs moved in and took chunks out of their legs. Sickly cries and screams of pain emerged from the ghostly faces of the pirate clan.

These pirates had not been affected by the illness, but still they were foul and rancid as they came up close.

Three skeletal fiends pounced on Stanley and pinned him to the floor. A fourth approached with something heavy, about to bring it down on the boy.

Thud. Good old Daisy. Armed with a pole, she brought the villain to the ground and then ran at the rest, holding it out lengthways. Three bony buccaneers fell like skittles, shattering into pieces.

But they reassembled themselves from their fragments, and the violent struggle continued.

The Angel tore through the crowd, leaving many injured. But it was the good fortune of Crampton Rock that he saw every man as his enemy, and soon he tore into the last of the pirates. They sensed that he had the ancient prize, and every one of them was drawn to him, but he cut into them so fast his triumph was effortless.

Then Stanley saw, as if in slow motion, a moment of suffering that appeared on Angel's face. Sweat was pouring from his brow, and it appeared as if his supernatural force was waning.

Perhaps he had given the fight all he had. Maybe his efforts had sapped all his energy. But no, it was not the fight that tired him, it was the fever. And now his sweat was black.

He had fought so hard all night and all day he had not stopped to notice that he too was ailing. His blade grew slower, his movements more shallow. The wolves grew slower too, panting and heaving, losing their appetite for blood.

The tide had turned. Now the gypsy blows came thick and fast.

In a final attempt to win the battle, Angel Cuzco raised his sword high to deal a fatal swipe to Stanley. But the mighty Bartley sent a crushing blow into the Angel's middle, and his bony carcass shattered into pieces and scattered over the ground. And as it did so the wolves fell too.

Angel Cuzco's broad cutlass dropped. Stanley had fallen, and the point of its blade landed perilously close to him. It pinned the collar of his shirt to the ground. He was so shaken that he seemed to lose consciousness.

He came around as he felt a tongue lashing across his face. It was one of the gypsy dogs, desperate to bring him back. He stroked its face and laughed, then jumped to his feet.

The enemy lay defeated on the ground. The whole of the gypsy encampment roared in triumph.

Stanley took a close look at his enemy. The light from the two emerald eyes was dying out like failing candles, turning to sheer black. His body and those of all the wolves turned from grisly festering skin to pure white bone in moments. And before long every scrap of proof that they had ever existed had wisped into the air. The only thing left was the shining silver amulet that they all knew to be the Ibis.

Stanley's eyes were drawn to it as it lay upon the ground. The Angel had found it after all, drawn to the hold of the ship, just as he had planned. He grasped it tightly and tucked it away in his pocket. He now knew that in the darkened privacy of Candlestick Hall, he was about to uncover the greatest secret in pirate history.

15

Unlocked

Phinn came to Stanley and then to Daisy, gathering them together. "Come and speak to Greta," he asked.

Stanley and Daisy followed him back to Greta's tent to the sound of cheers and roars. There would be a celebration soon, but they would need some sleep first. Stanley had been away from home for too long and he knew the consequences, but right now he was not too concerned. His biggest worries had been dealt with.

"Come in Stanley, Daisy," said Greta. "Have a drink, and take a moment to calm yourselves down."

They sat and talked a while, and soon they were laughing and joking. "Go on, Stanley," smiled Greta. "Take yourself home now—after all, you'll have some explaining to do when you get back. And we'll be happy for you to pay us a visit whenever you please. You too, Daisy."

So much had happened, yet Stanley and Daisy barely spoke on the way back. They were feeling shock or exhaustion, or a combination of both. They stopped every now and then and stared at the peaceful harbor. They were on their way back to reality.

They entered the house through the old coal bin, hoping to sneak in unnoticed and pretend they had been around for some time. In theory it was a good plan, but when they'd climbed in they could hear the adults in the kitchen. It was twice as hard to avoid detection now that Mrs. Carelli had Victor back.

Stanley and Daisy could hear the Carellis in full discussion about their whereabouts. And then, a stroke of luck: it sounded as if they were putting on their coats and heading out to find them.

Good. Time to move through the house.

In they sneaked, like bilge rats slinking over

the ballast of the ship, lurking and snooping, then darting through the winding corridors until they arrived safely in the comfort of Stanley's room.

With bated breath, they placed the silver casket on the chest under the window. Stanley fumbled in his pocket for the cloth-covered Ibis. She did not bear any scars, despite her long journey since she left the comfort of the pike's belly.

Stanley flicked out the two prongs at the back of the Ibis. His great-uncle, Admiral Swift, had explained this part to him, though he never thought he would see the day when the Ibis and the casket were reunited. Then Stanley lined her up with the empty space in the lock. He gently pushed it inward and waited until a neat click sounded.

Daisy looked at Stanley and Stanley looked

at Daisy. He turned the small horizontal bar until it was in a vertical position and it clicked again. Stanley felt the lid release its age-old grip, and they peered inside.

"Candles?" they both asked.

Stanley counted them. ". . . Four, five, six candles. Mmmmm."

He and Daisy took them out and stared at them for a good while. There was nothing special about them, or at least it didn't seem as though there was. After all, they were only wax. No sign or special mark about them except for a small"C" stamped in the base of each one.

The casket alone was enough to set their hearts alight, but the candles were a mystery.

"Perhaps there was nothing in particular inside it, so someone thought it was a good place to store things?" suggested Daisy.

"Maybe," said Stanley. It didn't matter. To see the casket complete was more than they could have hoped for. Who cared what lay inside.

Later, he found the perfect place for the silver casket. He put it behind the false panel in his cupboard, and it was safely out of sight. After all, he did not know when sinister company would next throw a shadow across his door.

16

Beyond the Candlelight

The children were foolish to think they could avoid the adults forever, and that night Stanley had to endure a dreadful argument. He was in serious trouble, confined to his room.

Disappearing for days at a time! Nowhere to be seen! No messages left! Nothing! Mrs. Carelli couldn't cope with it. It would have to stop.

Daisy was sent home and suffered equally when she returned to her aunt and uncle.

Stanley knew he would have to weather the storm and wait until Mrs. Carelli's anger had blown over.

He spent hours looking over the intricacies of the silver casket. However closely he looked, there was always something new to see. Strange patterns and shapes; little heads of lions; the claws and tails of slinking lizards, each of them like a tiny silver gargoyle, winding their way around the casket almost as if they were alive.

The good thing about his confinement to the house was that he could closely watch over this ancient treasure. Besides, there were always adventures to be had inside. He could live there forever and still occasionally find a new doorway.

It was a perfect day. The sun broke across the harbor, and it was low tide. For once Crampton Rock really was peaceful.

Victor had taken up his new role in the

house marvelously. He was out pruning the trees and clipping the lawn while Mrs. Carelli was busy creating something in the kitchen.

"It's a nice day!" said Stanley, with his eyes gazing expectantly at Mrs. Carelli.

"Go on then," she said, giving in. "You can go out. Just as long as you don't disappear."

"I won't," he answered. He decided he would take a little time to help Victor, and maybe get to know him better.

Picking up some pruning shears, he began to make a mess of things.

"Here, son," came Victor's voice. "Like this." In his gentle way he took the time to show Stanley what to do, and soon they were like old friends, chatting away and working together.

Mrs. Carelli looked out of the kitchen window. It was years since she had watched

Victor as he tidied the rose beds or raked the grass in their own little garden back in the village. His hair had turned to white in the time he had been missing, and he was much thinner than he'd ever been.

She shrugged off a single tear and went back to her work with a smile.

Out in the yard, Stanley and Victor were locked in conversation. "Have you always lived here?" Stanley questioned.

"My family have been here for years. My father, my father's father, and his father before him. All of us continued the business in the village, one after the other."

"Were you fishermen?"

"Oh no, son. We were candle makers. The old shop still sits in the village, but the door has not been opened since I left the island all those years ago. Violet could not bring herself

to go there
while I was
gone, so she
took the job as
housekeeper for
Admiral Swift.
Perhaps I will
return there
some day soon."

"I see. And do you mind if I ask you about the pirates who attacked you?" asked Stanley.

"Well, I guess I don't mind. I haven't really talked about it too much."

Stanley detected a note of sadness in his voice. "Perhaps we should talk of something else," he suggested. He had no intention of upsetting poor Victor.

"Not at all," said Victor. "It'll do me good to

speak of it. I should not harbor the memory all to myself."

And he began.

"I'd set out one afternoon when the tide had lifted the boats in the harbor, intending to go fishing. I had candles for a small island that sits north-west of here and I thought I would see what I could catch on the way. I had only reached the west coast of Crampton Rock, just short of Scarecrow Point, when they appeared.

"A real band of rogues they were. Their own vessel was bigger than mine, much bigger, and they saw that I was alone. I was an easy target. They approached me and when they found out what I was carrying they came aboard and took my stock.

"They abandoned me on the island and cannonballed my boat to smithereens."

"I don't understand," said Stanley. "Why would pirates be interested in your candles?"

"Good question, Stanley but there is sound reasoning behind it. Believe it or not, candle trading is dangerous business where pirates dwell."

"Why on earth is that?" quizzed Stanley. "Well, when piracy was rife in these parts and treasures of one kind and another were passed from rogue to rogue and buried here and there, maps were hidden in all sorts of places.

"Many years ago, pirates knocked on the door of my father's shop in the dead of night. At gunpoint they forced him to make six candles. Each one concealed a rolled-up section of a large map.

"When they left, they were savaged by the werewolf as they escaped across the moor, and the candles disappeared. They were never found. I can only guess where they are now.

"The pirates from their crew did not believe in the werewolf, and we were blamed by them for the murders and for stealing the map. It made life hard for us. Eventually the mystery of the Carelli candles became notorious, and many came in search of them. Your Uncle Bart was one of them, Stanley, and although he was never to find them, he gave up his pirate life and bought Darkling Hall, renaming it Candlestick Hall after his long search for the Carelli candles."

Stanley stood with eyes wide open.

"I promised you that one day I would repay you for your kindness. I hope that what I have told you is of help," Victor said, with a knowing look.

"Oh, it is, Victor. It really is." Stanley smiled at him, then cleared away his tools and set off back into the house.

There was something he had to do.